Down in the Woods at Sleepytime

For all of my big and little friends at
Little Friends, especially Debbie, Rosemary,
Barb, Kari, Brie, Becca, Eric, and Stefan
C. L. S.

For my family
V. C.

ISBN 0-439-31236-1

12 11 10 9 8 7 6 5 4 3 2 1   1 2 3 4 5 6/0

Printed in the U.S.A.   08

First Scholastic printing, October 2001

This book was typeset in Maiandra GD.
The illustrations were done in pencil and watercolor.

Down in the Woods at Sleepytime

Carole Lexa Schaefer illustrated by Vanessa Cabban

SCHOLASTIC INC.
New York Toronto London Auckland Sydney
Mexico City New Delhi Hong Kong Buenos Aires

Deep down in the woods,
Mama Bear says, "It's sleepytime."

"No, uh-uh," grumble her cubs.
"We still want to play."

And they clown around

in the scruffy brush.

Deep down in the woods,
Mama Hedgehog says, "It's sleepytime."

"No, uh-uh," squeal her prickly babies.
"We're still hungry."

And they snuffle for snacks

in the mossy grass.

Deep down in the woods,
Mama Rabbit says, "It's sleepytime."

"No, uh-uh," squeak her bunnies.
"We're still peek-a-booing."

And hip-hop, they hide

under fat, green leaves.

Deep down in the woods,
Mama Toad says, "It's sleepytime."

"No, hmm-mmm," hum her toadlets.
"We're still making up songs."

And "Hmm goo, mmm blup,"

they sing from the top of their log.

Deep down in the woods,
on her branch above them all,
wise Grandma Owl hoots,

"Whoo-hoo!

It's storytime."

And she begins.

"Deep down in the woods,
bear cubs are nestling,
cozy in the
leaves,

baby hedgehogs are
curling into tight,
warm balls,

bunnies snuggle
close to each
other,

and toadlets settle
softly in the
goo glup
mud...."

Wise Grandma Owl
blinks her big eyes.
She looks around....

"Whoo-hoo," hoots wise Grandma Owl.

"Sweet

dreams."